First U.S. edition 2006

Library of Congress Cataloging-in-Publication Data is available.

Library of Congress Catalog Card Number 2005053183

ISBN 0-7636-3063-2

10 9 8 7 6 5 4 3 2 1

Printed in Singapore

This book was typeset in Goudy.

The illustrations were done in watercolor and pencil.

Candlewick Press, 2067 Massachusetts Avenue, Cambridge, Massachusetts 02140

visit us at www.candlewick.com

MIA'S STORY

A Sketchbook of Hopes and Dreams by

MICHAEL FOREMAN

CANDLEWICK PRESS

CAMBRIDGE, MASSACHUSETTS

I will never forget the day I met Mia. My bus
had broken down, and I found myself in her village.
We made friends at once, and I want
to tell you about her. This is Mia's story.

Mia's village is called Campamento San Francisco and is somewhere between the big city and the snowy mountains. It is not much of a place. But for Mia it is her home and her world.

There are no pretty gardens or trees.
There isn't a proper road, just a muddy track.

Mia's papa and his truck

He goes to the city every day to sell scrap.

It used to be farmland, but the city grew bigger and bigger, and now they can only harvest what the city throws away.

This is Mia's house.

Mia's mama

The houses are made from odds and ends and bits of trash, whatever the people can find.

nia's school

The children love playing soccer.

These are the ovens where the villagers bake their bread.

They are very clever at fixing things they find in the dump.

Sometimes Papa comes home happy
with money in his pockets,
and sometimes he comes home sad
with none.

Mia runs to meet her papa
every evening.

Mia's father dreams of one day being
able to build a house of bricks.

One evening in early autumn, Mia's father came home with a strange grin on his face. He unzipped his jacket, and there was a beautiful puppy! Papa had found him all alone in the city.

Mia kissed her new puppy on the nose. She decided to call him Poco because he was so small.

Mia showed the puppy
to everyone, and soon he
was part of her life.

*Poco likes his
new family.*

*Poco licks Mia's face,
then Mama's face,
and then Papa's face.*

Mia shows Poco to Sancho.

Hello, Sancho!

Poco follows Mia everywhere — even to school.

He is very good and waits outside until the end of lessons.

But it was a hard winter, and one day Poco disappeared. Mia searched the village, then she climbed onto Sancho and set off to look through the dump.

A pack of dogs went that way. He could have been with them.

Have you seen my little dog?

He is small and brown and patchy.

Come on, Sancho. We'll find him.

Poco! Poco!

As she searched, she got farther and farther from home . . .

until eventually she found herself
high up in the mountains, far higher
than she had been before. From
up there she could look down
on the dark cloud
that always filled
the valley.

The air above the cloud was so clean it took Mia's breath away. She was dazzled by the whiteness all around. She jumped down from Sancho and grabbed the snow, tasting it and rolling over and over in the whole white world of it.

Sancho watched her, and then he too rolled over and kicked his old legs in the air. Then Mia lay on her back, arms and legs outstretched in the snow. The sky had never been so blue and so near.

She called and searched for Poco until night began
to fall and the first stars appeared. Mia was exhausted,
but she knew that Sancho would take her safely home.

They set off slowly until suddenly he stopped and
snuffled at the ground. Mia looked around. Instead of
snow, they were now surrounded by flowers. Mia
carefully gathered a clump, roots and all. She knew
that whatever happened, they would remind her of how
she looked for Poco and found this place in the stars.

The next day, Mia planted the flowers.

She pots some in tin cans.

She tends them and waters them everyday.

The flowers grow tall
and strong, and they
spread in the summer.

In the autumn, the wind
blows seeds all over the village.

The flowers spread quickly. By the following spring, they had spread all over the village, and the dump was covered with flowers as white as the mountain snow.

Although she enjoyed looking after the flowers, Mia never forgot Poco and called for him every day.

One morning when her father was leaving for the city with a load of scrap to sell, Mia said she wanted to go with him to try and sell her flowers. She pointed to rows of white flowers in tin cans. Her father laughed and agreed to give it a try.

Mia put her flowers on the steps of the cathedral,
and Papa laid out his scrap nearby.

The main square is busy
with traders.

Rain or
shine.

There are always lots
of musicians.

What a beautiful
baby!

Not sold much
today?

Soon Mia had so many customers,
Papa had to give up his scrap business to
help sell flowers. People asked, "Where
do these flowers come from?"
And Mia said, "They come
from the stars."

From that day on, Mia and Papa sold flowers and shared his
dream of building a house of bricks. And whenever a pack
of dogs came running by, Mia thought of Poco . . .

until one day one of the dogs stopped running
and came to smell the flowers. He licked
Mia's face and lay down among them.

for Manuel and his family.
may you have a house of bricks
one day.